Wizzy-Woo and his Brand New Friends

by Helga Hopkins
Illustrated by Debbie Clark

First published 2007
Second Edition published 2019
Contact: info@wizzywoo.com

ISBN: 9781795402385

wizzy-woo™
and his brand new friends

Helga Hopkins
illustrated by Debbie Clark

Wizzy Woo and his Brand New Friends

Wizzy-Woo is a little honey-coloured kitten. He was born on a beautiful summer's day in a great big haystack beside a farmyard.

A few days later, his mum carried him across the farmyard to the farmhouse. Lots of big dogs and cats and other animals lived there, and it was a very dangerous place for a little kitten to be.

To protect Wizzy, the farmer's wife put him in a rabbit hutch. Wizzy didn't like that one bit.

It was very boring. All he wanted to do was explore, and have some exciting adventures like the big cats did.

One morning when the farmer's wife was feeding Wizzy, she told him: 'You're going to have a visitor today. A lady is coming to have a look at you because she wants a kitten for her little girl.
I hope she'll like you'.

'I'll make SURE she likes me', thought Wizzy. 'I must get out of this rabbit hutch!' So when the farmer's wife put Wizzy in the visitors arms, he was as charming as he could be. Wizzy started to purr very loudly and licked the lady's face for all he was worth!

'Oh, what a lovely sweet kitten!' the lady said. 'I'll take him home with me right now'.

'And that's the last I'll see of that rabbit hutch,'
whispered Wizzy to himself.

When they arrived at her house, the lady introduced him to his new owner - a sweet little girl called Kristin. She gave him a big hug and a few delicious cat treats. Wizzy had never dreamed that life could be so good!

During the night he had a lovely soft cat bed to sleep in, but felt very lonely and desperately wanted to be with Kristin.

So he crept up the steep stairs and gingerly jumped on Kristin's bed and snuggled up in the little girl's arms.

Wizzy soon fell fast asleep and dreamed of never-ending cat treats.

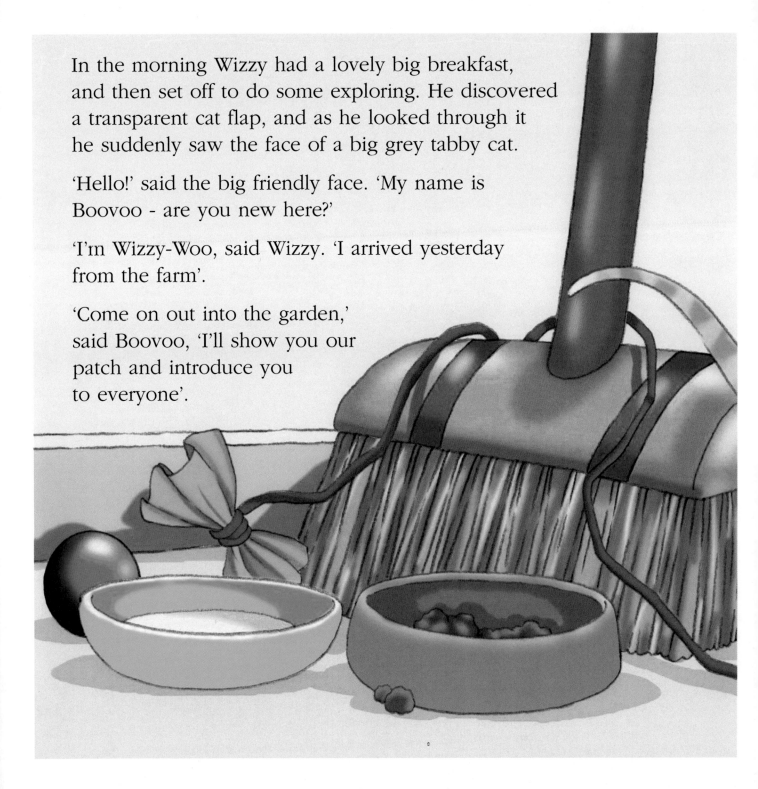

In the morning Wizzy had a lovely big breakfast, and then set off to do some exploring. He discovered a transparent cat flap, and as he looked through it he suddenly saw the face of a big grey tabby cat.

'Hello!' said the big friendly face. 'My name is Boovoo - are you new here?'

'I'm Wizzy-Woo, said Wizzy. 'I arrived yesterday from the farm'.

'Come on out into the garden,' said Boovoo, 'I'll show you our patch and introduce you to everyone'.

Wizzy cautiously poked his little head through the door and climbed out. 'Over there behind the fence lives Bivitt - he's grey with white feet, and you'd better avoid him as he doesn't like little kittens like you,' said Boovoo. 'Our girl-cat friends Sylvia and Squeeze live next door'.

'Sylvia is a very naughty kitten and is always in trouble. Squeeze is only interested in licking herself and looking as pretty as possible'.

Wizzy was very excited and couldn't wait to meet up with Sylvia and start having some of those exciting adventures.

Next morning, Wizzy heard a strange noise coming from the kitchen. A small kitten had climbed through the cat flap and was examining Wizzy's new toy box. This was obviously Sylvia.

Wizzy boldly introduced himself and suggested that they both set off on an adventure together.

Sylvia wanted to take a look at the neighbour's goldfish, and while they were looking into the pond they suddenly heard a noise behind them.

'Now what are you young kittens doing on my territory?' said Bivitt, who was huge and was angrily creeping up behind them.

'Look out, 'Sylvia whispered. 'We mustn't let him catch us!'
And with that she quickly led Wizzy out onto the giant pond leaves.

'You two are not going to escape that easily!' growled Bivitt, who promptly took a mighty jump onto the first watery leaf.

The leaves were just strong enough to carry two little kittens, but certainly not a big heavy cat. All of a sudden, the big leaf folded around Bivitt, and he disappeared under the water in a spray of coloured bubbles.

'You'd better come off the pond and forget your adventures for today,' said Boovoo, watching from the safety of the fence.

'And be very careful, because Bivitt will be angry and looking for revenge'.

Next morning there was a frantic knocking on the cat flap.
It was Sylvia, completely out of breath. 'Bivitt has Squeeze
cornered in the garden!' She panted.

'We have to help her, as she has no idea how to
help herself!'

Wizzy and Sylvia raced out to help, but
they were just too late.

In sheer fright, Squeeze had climbed up
a big high fir tree, and was much too
afraid to come down again.

'We've got to get Boovoo to help us,' said Wizzy. But when they asked him, the kind old cat just couldn't think how to help. 'Squeeze will never be able to get down on her own,' he said. We'll just have to get the humans to help out'.

'But how?' said Sylvia, 'the humans are stupid and don't understand us'. So all three cats thought very hard and scratched their chins.

Just then they heard Kristin singing and skipping in the garden. 'Get her to follow you and lead her to Squeeze,' Boovoo cried.

'I always get the difficult jobs' muttered Wizzy. But then he had a brilliant idea! 'If I pretend to be lost, Kristin will come and look for me'.

So Wizzy meowed loudly from behind the fence, and Kristin hurried over.

'Hurry up, Wizzy!' shouted Sylvia' 'or Kristin will catch you up before you get to Squeeze!'

Wizzy was too out of breath to give an answer, but with a little help from Boovoo, he struggled up and over the garden fence towards the tree where Squeeze was stuck.

'Oh no, look!' said Kristin, 'Squeeze is stuck up the tree - let's get the fireman to save her with his ladder'.

In no time at all, Squeeze was safely in the fireman's arms, and Wizzy and the others gave a big sigh of relief.

'What an exciting day it's been!' said Kristin, scooping Wizzy up over her head. 'I think you deserve some lovely cooked fish for dinner tonight'. Wizzy twirled his little ginger ears with pleasure and licked Kristin on the nose.

'Oh - and don't worry!' said Kristin, smiling at Sylvia and Squeeze. 'Fish for you two as well!'

... and Wizzy-Woo says, 'Watch out for my next adventure!'

Made in the USA
Middletown, DE
19 May 2020